RESOLUTION REVOLUTION

CAPRICORN COVE SERIES

EVIE MITCHELL

THUNDER THIGHS PUBLISHING

Editor: Nicole Wilson, Evermore Editing
http://www.evermoreediting.wixsite.com/info

ACKNOWLEDGEMENT OF COUNTRY

I acknowledge the Traditional Custodians of the lands on which I write, the Ngunnawal people, and pay my respect to elders both past and present.

I acknowledge the continued and deep spiritual relationship of the Australian Aboriginal and Torres Strait Islander peoples' to this land, and their unique cultural and spiritual relationships to the land, waters and seas and their rich contribution to society.

Always was, always will be.

To my Greedy Readers – you are all equally the best!
And to my husband, for challenging me to do things I never thought possible... like climb mountains in Italy while recovering from food poisoning.
NEVER. AGAIN!

RESOLUTION REVOLUTION

Karen

Have you ever had a meme made of your name? I have. Every single day. It's what people think about before they even meet me. "Oh, she's such a Karen." Charming.

In part, that's why I keep to myself, hiding behind my microphone as the voice of The Wicked Women Podcast. Only this year, my producer wants to get me out of the studio and try new things.

So we make a set of new year's resolutions, which includes me being forced out into the world.

I hate the world. The world sucks.

Or at least it did before I met Will. I find I quite like the world when it involves the owner of our local lumber company.

And I'm discovering a new interest in hardwoods.

Will

Who thought a zip-lining corporate bonding experience would turn into finding the love of my life? Not me, that's for sure.

Karen is witty, intelligent, and utterly perfect.

I want her. Badly.

Only problem? She's way out of my league, and I'm just waiting for her to realise that.

Warning: This book contains hardwood. So get thee a lumberjack and settle in, cause this new year romance is about to start off with a bang!

1

Karen

"Hey, all you Pretty Pollys out there, welcome to the first episode of the Wicked Women podcast for the new year. I'm Karen Q, and I'm here with my co-host—"

"Mistress H."

"—to discuss all things feminist, feminine, and fine as fuck!"

I hit the play button on the sound desk, nodding in time to the intro music. On the other end of the screen, my co-host, Hannah Sharp, tilted her head to the side, her lips moving as she counted down to the end of the tune. Unlike me, in my sloppy PJs and bed-hair, Hannah looked as neat as a pin, her white pantsuit perfectly pressed, her blonde hair cascading around her shoulders in perfectly positioned beach curls.

It's nice that some things in life are predictable.

"Mistress H, tell me, how were your holidays? Did you conquer the dreaded Christmas family dinner?"

Hannah sighed, shaking her head. "No. Despite all efforts to be civil, dinner disintegrated into a melee of words between my father, his new girlfriend, and my aunt."

I winced. "Ouch. Was it entertaining, at least?"

"For the first two hours, then the cops arrived. After that, it was just me attempting to bail my aunt out of jail and dealing with paperwork for the next six hours."

I hit the sad sound button. "That sounds like the worst Christmas you've had since the one where someone ate your dessert."

"It was. At least this time, I got pudding."

We chatted about our holidays, filling our listeners in on what was happening in our lives before cutting to a commercial break.

"And we're back," I said into the microphone, repositioning my earphones. "It's time to introduce our guest for this week. She's our producer, a mom-to-be, a kickass boss lady, and one of the best friends I've ever had. Let's give it up for Christine!"

I hit the button to add cheers, grinning as I unmuted the screen.

"Chrissy-boo, how are you?" I asked, blowing her air kisses.

"Fat, fun, and fine as fuck." She laughed, holding her hand up to the screen for a high-five. I pretended to air-smack her palm, laughing at Hannah's eye roll.

"May I remind you that you're pregnant?" Hannah asked with a flick of her hair. "Fat is not a descriptor I'd use for the beauty of your body right now."

"Mistress, I love you, but you are dead wrong." Christine leaned back, patting her eight-month-pregnant belly. "I am so done with being pregnant. It feels as if my ankles are about to explode. If I don't get some foot massages up in here, I'm worried I may never walk again."

"I'd just like to remind you of something you said at the start of this single mom journey. What was it? Oh, that's right." I grinned, making my voice wispy and overly high-pitched. "Pregnancy is a gift, and I can't wait to experience it all. And best of all, I don't have to share it with anyone else."

Chrissy groaned. "I hate that you remember that."

"Babe, I remember everything."

We all cackled before Hannah sobered, lifting her clipboard to check the run schedule.

"Chrissy, your email was incredibly cryptic. All it says is that you want to talk to us about resolutions."

"Uh-huh." She leaned forward, grinning into the computer screen. "I've decided it's time to shake up this little podcast. You ladies have had enough of being safe at home hiding behind your microphones. I've decided it's time to get you out from behind the desk and into the big bad world."

I blinked. "Huh?"

Hannah, always more articulate than me, clarified, "What are you asking us to do?"

Christine rubbed her hands together. "I've signed you both up for a few new year's resolutions."

"What?"

"Why?"

"You can't do that!"

"This is a horrible idea!"

"I hate people!"

"You know Karen hates people."

She made a quiet motion with her hands. "Look, I get it. It's a big scary world filled with people you might hate. But ladies, you're Wicked Women. And Wicked Women don't settle. They don't stay at home when there are challenges to be slain. They get out there and take names. And that's what I want you to do."

She clicked her screen, sharing it with us. "I asked the listeners over the holidays to send us their bucket lists. From that, I've pulled the things that are in the local area. Over the next few months, we're going to tick them off one by one."

I could feel my eyebrows disappearing into my hairline. "I'm sorry, does that say zip-lining?"

"What exactly is a Brazilian cleanse?" Hannah asked, frowning at the screen.

"Patience ladies, let me explain." Christine leaned into her microphone, dropping her voice an octave. "You'll thank me later."

I doubt it.

"I've signed you both up for things that I think you need. Mistress, you need more self-care, more vulnerability, more emotion, and more lightness in your life."

Hannah's lips pressed together, a frown creasing her forehead. "Do I?"

"Yes." Christine gave a firm nod. "You do. That's why we've signed you up for different types of relaxation and emotional connection classes."

"But... meat load therapy? What is that? Is that an actual activity or a cooking class?"

"Oh, it looks amazing!" Christine enthused. "It's a new spa therapy that involves wrapping yourself in fur while a piece of steak is placed over your face. You then listen to the sounds of the forest while meditating. Apparently, it's very primal."

There was a beat of silence.

"Let me get this straight. Mistress H is becoming a shish kebab while I try my luck at being a daredevil?" I asked, staring at the list of feats I apparently needed to achieve. "Chrissy, this reads like a list of ways to die. I mean, skydiving? Fuck. No."

She grinned. "I thought you'd say that, that's why I've already pre-purchased everything. All you need to do is turn up."

Stunned silence met her declaration.

I coughed, my voice hoarse. "I'm sorry. Can you repeat that?"

"All you need to do is turn up. All the details are in your emails right now."

Hannah and I stared at each other via the computer screen.

"Mistress H, any thoughts?" I asked.

Hannah closed her eyes, sucking in a deep breath before slowly letting it out. "I don't like surprises."

"Psh." Chrissy waved a dismissive hand. "Surprises are awesome."

"And," Hannah continued. "I don't like being touched. This sounds like something *you* want, Christine. Not Karen or I."

Again, Christine dismissed her. "You'll enjoy it if you give it a chance."

Hannah sucked in a breath, her face turning into what I liked to call her *don't fuck with me* expression.

Sock it to her, Hannah!

"Christine," she began, her voice ice cold. "As you would be aware, consent is not something limited to sexual activity. It crosses all lines. In this instance, while you've offered something that sounds wonderful, you didn't seek consent to undertake this kind of decision. It's one thing to surprise someone. It's quite another to not accept that they don't wish to do it."

There was a moment of silence from Chrissy.

I leaned forward, whispering into the microphone, "Hard burn from Mistress H. Let's see how Chrissy retaliates."

Christine slowly shook her head. "So, you're saying I've overstepped?"

"Yes."

Chrissy's eyes narrowed on Hannah. "Excuse me?"

"You made a decision—"

"You told me you were up for an adventure!"

"I thought you meant one activity! One! And something that wouldn't involve touching!"

The discussion disintegrated from there. I slowly turned down their mics, allowing their bickering to become a background to my voice-over.

"And that, dearest listener, is the reason we don't surprise Mistress H. Ever. We'll be back, right after these messages from our sponsors."

I hit the play button, switching us all off record. I'd clean up our sound before uploading it to the various platforms.

"Guys," I called, trying to get their attention. "Ladies!"

They fell silent, their two-dimensional faces mutinous on the computer screen.

"What if we just give it a go?" I asked. "I mean, I could try—" I checked the list, swallowing against the bad taste in my mouth. "Zip-lining. And I could take one of the massages. Maybe between the both of us, we could just work out what we want to do."

Hannah exhaled, that familiar ice settling across her features—impenetrable and protective, safely hiding away her true thoughts.

"That will be fine."

"Except for the meat load therapy," Chrissy

said, waggling a finger at the screen. "That one is non-transferable."

"Fine, I shall be decked out in meat while listening to jungle sounds. Are you satisfied?"

Chrissy, well used to Hannah's still protectionist voice, laughed. "Yep."

"And Chrissy, next time you have a great idea like this, what will you do?"

She rolled her eyes at me. "I'll ask first. Even if I think it's for your own good."

"Thank you."

The prerecorded ads ended, and I leaned back into the microphone. "Alright, so it's settled. We're off to zip-lining and meat therapy. Listeners, wish us luck 'cause Mistress H and I are pretty sure we're about to die."

2

Karen

I glanced from my phone to the sign, squinting at the notification on the bottom, then back down to the waiver on my phone once again.

"Well shit."

I didn't know what to expect when I'd rocked up at the zip-lining place, but this certainly wasn't it.

INHERENT HAZARDS and risks include but are not limited to:

- Risk of injury from the activity and equipment, including the potential

> for significant and/or permanent disability and death.
> - Possible equipment failure and/or malfunction of my own or other's equipment.
> - Attack by or encounter with insects, reptiles, and/or other animals.
> - Accidents or illnesses occurring in remote places where there are no available medical facilities....

The list went on and on.

"You okay, Karen?"

I swallowed, looking up at the dreamy man whose wedding ring glinted in the morning sun. Drake Andrews had to be one of the most attractive men I'd ever met.

"Um, yep."

He grinned, and my heart sighed.

"Look, it's a technical waiver, but we've had no major injuries beyond a few strains and bruises. We've been here for nearly five years now, and, God willing, we'll never have a serious injury. Dane and I are trained professionals. Don't worry, we've got you."

I nodded, butterflies the size of jet planes still flapping in my stomach.

"Right. Of course." I signed the waiver,

handing it back to him. "Is it just you and me today?"

He checked my answers, making a small note in one of the margins. "Actually, you're a little early. The rest of the crew hasn't arrived yet."

"Oh."

He looked up, his friendly grin still in place. "How about we take you inside and get you kitted up, that way you can relax with some coffee while we wait."

"Um, sure."

I followed him into a large barn that had been converted into a classroom and storage for the multitudes of equipment. The place felt surprisingly modern despite the wood.

"Do you mind if I take a picture and start recording this?" I asked, holding up my spare phone. "It's for the—"

"Wicked Women podcast." Drake grinned. "Your producer told us when she booked it. And if we hadn't known then, our wife would have told us."

"Our?"

"Mine and his," a gruff voice said behind me. I twisted, looking over my shoulder to see another delicious man enter the barn. He held out a hand for me to shake.

"I'm Dane."

Where Drake was all light, Dane was all darkness.

"Lovely to meet you."

He gripped my hand, giving it a warm, solid shake.

And damn, wish I was as lucky as their wife. Two men? Gr-owl!

"Is your wife joining us?"

They both laughed.

"Nope," Drake said, still chuckling as he pulled a harness and helmet from the wall. "She's petrified of heights. Won't even go into the hayloft for fear of falling."

I tilted my head back, grimacing as I took in the solid ladder that led up into the converted loft space. "I feel her."

"Uh-oh." Drake shook his head. "Don't tell me you're scared of heights."

"Only like ninety-nine-point-nine percent of the time."

They both sighed, shaking their heads in unison.

"Right, let's get you fitted."

Drake handed me a harness, explaining how to put it on as he watched. Behind him, Dane checked the rest of the equipment, making notes on his tablet as he went.

"Now, I'll just tighten this for you." Drake reached over, tightening the straps. "What we want is tight but not strangulation. You need room to move and not get pinched by the harness." He stepped back, gesturing at the straps. "How's that?"

I gave a little shimmy, walking a few steps and then giving him a nod. "Feels good."

"Great. Now have a go climbing the ladder over there, just a few rungs, we want to see that it's not riding up or falling down anywhere it shouldn't."

I blinked. "Sorry, what?"

He gestured at the ladder. "Just over there."

Silently cursing Chrissy, I moved to the ladder, trying desperately not to look like a fool as I began to scramble up the rungs.

"Hey, is this the right place for zip-lining?"

I glanced over my shoulder and died. I actually felt my spirit leave my body as I stared in horror at the three men clustered in the doorway, all of whom were, in turn, staring at my ass.

To be fair, the only exercise clothing I owned involved novelty-themed leggings, so maybe they were staring at the baby Yoda faces decorating my lower half... but still... dead.

"Yep, come on in." Drake gestured them over.

"We're just getting your fourth member for today sorted. I'll be right with you."

My head twisted around, and I stared at my hands where they clutched at the wooden rung, a flush working its way up my neck to burn like the lava on my cheeks.

"Hey, Karen? You okay up there?"

You mean apart from the mortification?

I nodded, sucking in a breath then began the climb back down. "Yep, fine."

Back on the ground, I found Dane handing out harnesses and helmets.

"Feels like work, hey boss?" one of the younger guys cracked to the older man in their group.

"Only, I have to put up with your crap today," the guy with the attractive salt and pepper hair cracked back.

"Guys, this is Karen. She's gonna be with us today as we explore the caves."

A record screeched in my head.

"C-c-caves?" I sputtered, staring at Drake.

"Yeah. We'll start with the tree course to get you familiar with it all, then move into the caves."

Chrissy is dead. She's worse than dead. She's going to be chopped into 1000 pieces and strewn about the cave so the bats can eat her.

"Okay, not what I was expecting, th-that's fine." I swallowed. "I got this, I mean, how hard can it be?"

Around me, the men chuckled but didn't answer.

"Hey, I'm Will. " Salt-and-pepper hottie held out his hand. I took it, giving it a firm shake, noting with approval the warmth and strength of his grip and the delicious callouses that rasped against my palm.

I must have died and gone to lumberjack heaven. 'Cause this guy is an absolute dish!

"Karen," I replied, feeling strangely breathy.

"Oh no," one of his boys muttered.

"Jay," Will warned, shooting him a look. The younger guy had tattoos up and down one arm, and his hair, now covered by a helmet, had been a short mohawk. He looked like the kids I'd gone to school with back in the day, Emos that had listened to metal and been the ones drinking in the car park after school.

I'd always wished I was brave enough to join them.

"Don't worry, I get it all the time. Your name becomes a meme, and suddenly you're the em-bodiment of it without even opening your mouth."

The kid had the grace to blush. "Sorry. I should know better than to judge."

"Yeah, looking at him, you'd expect him to have more brains." The third guy had to be closer to my age, maybe a few years younger, but not by much. "I'm Liam."

I shook his hand, grinning as he elbowed Jay.

"Nice to meet you all. Looks like I'll be tagging along for your boy's trip. Sorry."

Drake smoothly inserted himself in. "Don't apologise. Having even numbers makes it easier on me. Shall we get started?"

They signed the waivers, finished getting suited up, and I wrangled their permission to record them for the podcast before we headed outside to the beginner tree course, where I found myself sandwiched between Will and Jay as we listened to the briefing. Drake took his time explaining in detail the various activities we'd be undertaking and what we could expect from the course.

"Now, I'm going to be using a lot of rhyming today, so prepare yourself," Drake said with a grin. "First things first, these are the orange lifelines, and you must remain connected to them at all times. So how do we do this? Simple, we grip and clip."

The orange lifeline was a small metal hook that was embedded in the wood. To climb safely, you had to clip yourself to the lifeline, take a step, then clip the carabiner on the second line to the small metal loop, and so on and so forth.

"Let's partner up. We're gonna practice everything you just learned."

Will turned to me with a gorgeous smile. "Partner?"

I grinned, feeling a flutter of attraction. "Sounds like a plan."

We started off on small platforms, and I could tell immediately that these guys were experienced. Jay and Liam scrambled up the platforms, gripping and clipping like pros.

"They've done this before," I muttered, my heart thumping loudly in my chest as I watched them scramble across the balance bridge.

Beside me, Will chuckled.

"What do you guys do?"

"I own a lumberyard and sawmill. We specialise in sustainable timber harvesting."

Well, I certainly picked that.

I tilted my head to the side as above us, Jay and Liam traded insults. "Sustainable?"

He grinned. "Everyone hears sawmill and thinks of us cutting down large tracts of land willy-nilly. What we actually do is own plantations where we circulate the tree growth. When a plantation is mature, we cut it down and replant it a year or so later once the land has recovered. We offer removal for fallen trees, and we do clearing for roads and houses—this allows us to ensure the trees are harvested in a way that means every part will be used."

I nodded, impressed by his passion.

"We also recover used wood and timbers from cabins, train tracks, decks, and so on."

"Does timber ever reach an end of life?"

"Oh sure," he laughed. "Might be that the offcuts are tiny, or the wood is rotten. So we either turn it into something like a carving that can be sold, or we mulch it for use in gardens."

"Wow. I have to admit, I've never given hardwood that much thought."

"Phrasing!" Jay yelled from above us.

We both laughed, my face flushing a tiny bit.

"How about you? You said you're a podcaster. What's that like?"

We chatted about my job as we waited for Jay and Liam to get through the first obstacle.

"You're up. Take it slow, we're in no hurry," Dane assured me as his husband stood at the top of the platform, watching like a hawk as I clipped on.

Shit.

With a shaky breath and even shakier hands, I began the climb up to the first platform.

It only stood about ten feet off the ground, but that was enough to make me want to puke.

"You can do this, Karen," I muttered to myself as I shimmied along. "You've got this. You are a badass. You're a wicked woman. You—"

My foot slipped, a startled noise ripping from my throat as I tumbled back a step only to fall into the arms of Will.

"Don't worry. I've got you." His arms were clamped firmly around me. His body was warm and hard as he held me.

"Um." I tilted my head back. "Thanks."

"Anytime."

Will helped me settle back on the ladder, helping me readjust my grip, staying close while I began to climb—it felt nice to have someone watching my back.

"You okay?" Drake asked as I got to the top of the platform, attempting to gracefully heave myself up.

"Yeah, sorry. Didn't mean to freak out."

He grinned, wrapping his hands around my biceps and helping me stand. "Don't worry about it. We had a guy faint last month. Six-foot-two, built like a line-backer, petrified of heights. Took four of us to get him back to the ground. You're doing great."

"You are," Will confirmed, his biceps flexing

attractively as he pushed himself up. "I'd hire you."

I laughed, flattered by his flirty tone. "Thanks for the vote of confidence."

Drake and Dane put us through our paces, ensuring we were all safe and comfortable working at heights and with the equipment.

"Okay, now it's time to actually glide. Because this is your first time, Dane or I will set up your pulley for you." He demonstrated how to do it while Will hitched his up in such a way I knew it wasn't his first time.

"Now, sit down in your harness, place one hand here and wrap your other around it." Drake nodded when I did as directed. "Perfect. Now lean back, we don't want you getting your hair caught, keep your feet in front of you, then just ride it out."

I watched Will lean back in his harness, sliding easily between the two platforms.

"Oh God," I breathed, feeling the panic claw up my throat. "I don't think I can do this."

Will landed, standing on the other platform and unclipping. He waved, offering me a giant grin.

"Come on, Karrie! You can do it!"

Karrie? That's... actually really cute. Why have I never thought of this before?

"Karen? You okay?" Drake asked beside me.

Oh, right. Giant drop. Riding on a zip-line. Terrified of heights. Gonna die. No biggie.

I sucked in a deep breath and tried to force myself to sit, to do as Drake had instructed, hands in place, legs up, leaning back.

Instead, I froze.

"Karen?"

I swallowed, looking up to see Will across the way.

"You got this, gorgeous. Keep your eyes on me. We'll do this together. Ready?"

I nodded, my body shaking as I kept my gaze locked on his.

"Okay, hands up, good. Now lean back, that's it, great job. Legs up, perfect and—"

I felt Drake's hand on the small of my back, giving me a small push.

"—here we go!"

I didn't scream. I could proudly say I didn't scream or faint or puke—we'll ignore the fact it was because my freeze response kicked in, and I was fairly sure I blacked out the entire ride.

One minute I was leaning back, feeling Drake push me, the next, I was in Will's arms, looking up into his piercing golden eyes.

"Well, hello there." His smile was devilishly gorgeous. "Well done, Karrie. You did it."

I looked down, finding my feet firmly

planted on the second platform, Drake shooting me thumbs up from across the gap.

"I... well. Damn." I let go of Will, taking a step back. "I did it."

"Yeah, you did." He held up a hand. "Great job."

I slapped it, enjoying the sting of the high-five.

3

Karen

Over a lunch of delicious sandwiches and fresh cookies, I interviewed Drake and Dane, learning their background and why they'd chosen to start an adventure park in Capricorn Cove.

"This has always been home."

I took their picture, sighing a little when I caught them kissing as they started checking our gear, readying it for our afternoon session in the caves.

If I was completely honest, watching their easy, loving relationship stirred something in me. A large part of me, the part I'd long ago locked away, wanted what they had—companionship, laughter, and the spark. It showed in every movement, every glance, the loving touches. But another part of me doubted it would ever happen. Here I stood, a forty-something-year-old woman who'd never even had a relationship that lasted beyond ten dates.

Not that you want one. You're perfectly happy being alone. And the things technology does these days...

Drake hip-checked Dane on the way to the van, throwing him a laugh.

But oh, to be loved like that.

Will took a seat beside me, dropping his plate to his lap as he settled in.

"Are you from Capricorn Cove, Karen?"

I considered him, finding the grey that peppered his hair and the laugh lines beside his eyes incredibly attractive. I put him at around mid-forties, with the look of a man who was comfortable in who he is and how he lives.

"No, I actually moved here a few years ago after living on the South Island for a few years."

"Ah, my eldest son is going to vet school down South. In Musou, heard of it?"

I shook my head as my gaze discreetly dropped to his ring finger, finding it empty.

No tan line. What does that even mean?

I cleared my throat. "I hope he likes it."

"Loves it. Though I miss him like crazy."

I grinned. "That's really sweet."

Will flushed, picking up a sandwich to munch, seemingly uncomfortable with my praise.

Okay, this guy is too much to resist. Ah-dork-able.

I searched around, wanting to continue our conversation but unsure of what to say to this beefcake of a man.

"Sorry, again, for earlier."

Will raised an eyebrow. "For falling for me?"

I laughed. "I more mean nearly crushing you, but yeah. Let's go with that."

"You?" He looked me over. "Nah. You've got the kind of curves I love. We should go out sometime."

We both froze, our gazes locking.

Did he just...?

4

Will

What did I just say?

I hadn't dated in years. Between work, the kids, and my ex-wife, I hadn't had the time or the inclination to put myself out there. My left hand did just fine, thank you very much.

And yet.... Here I was. Flirting with a woman in Yoda pants.

Help me, Obi-Wan. You're my only hope.

"For... for dinner?" Karen asked, her big green eyes wide.

"Yeah. If you'd like to."

Across the picnic table, Liam and Jay watched with varying degrees of amusement, no doubt planning how to torture me about this moment later.

"Um, I'd like that."

I grinned, nodding. "Great. Cool. I mean, awesome. How about tomorrow?"

What the fuck?

As my youngest son would say—I had no chill.

"Wow. You move fast." Karen, thankfully, was grinning. "I'd love to. But I need to check something with your colleagues first." She turned to Jay and Liam. "Is he a scammer? 'Cause I have to warn you, I have a long-lost prince of an uncle who is trying to send me millions. I'm sure if I tell him about this he'll organise a background check for me."

I relaxed, holding up my hands in surrender. "Hey, let's start with dinner and then see if the background check is worth your while."

Jay, never one to keep his mouth shut, interrupted. "I can vouch for him. Will practically raised me."

I shot him a warning glare which he ignored.

Typical.

Karen leaned forward, sending me a saucy grin as she gave Jay her full attention. "Oh really? Do tell."

Jay nodded enthusiastically. "Dogg fosters kids. Adopted some of them too."

"Dogg?"

"William Dogg, with a double g," I clarified.

"Of Dogg Wood Lumber." Jay tapped his chest. "I'm the Wood."

She looked at Liam. "And you?"

"I just work with these bastards." He elbowed Jay. "And I grew up with this mofo. He's right, Dogg's awesome."

Karen tilted her head to one side, her gaze straying to my ring finger.

"Divorced." I shook my head ruefully. "We were a teen marriage. Got pregnant at seventeen and divorced at eighteen. Was never gonna work. We both knew better but did it anyway—the power of parent pressure."

Karen made a sympathetic face. "I know it well. So including Jay and the vet, you have two sons?"

Fuck.

I normally saved this info until at least date ten.

"Actually, six," I admitted. "One genetic, four by choice." I flicked the bird at Jay. "And this fucker 'cause he refused to leave. Little shit."

Jay took a bow. "You're welcome."

"That's a lot of responsibility." Karen bit her lip. "How old are your kids?"

"Sons. All boys. My oldest, Hayden the vet, is twenty-six. Acts like a forty-year-old, though. Then there's Jay at—"

"A young and spritely twenty-three." Jay winked at me. "I'm the attractive one in the brood."

"Noted." She laughed, rolling her eyes.

"James is eighteen and off at college. Ash is fifteen, nearly sixteen, and already in college—the kid is a damned genius. I've also got Ryan, who's twelve, and Sam, my youngest, who's eight."

Karen stared at me for a beat, her eyes wide and slightly panicked. "Wow. I mean... wow. That's quite a spread of ages."

"Not to mention the foster kids," Liam commented, reaching for another sandwich. "There's always a pile of kids running around the house."

"Though none at the moment," I rushed to assure her. "But we're always ready if a kid needs a place."

"That's really lovely."

I felt a flush creep up my neck.

"You know," Liam said, licking his finger. "If you need a place for dinner, my sister owns a bar in town. The Bronze Horseman. Have you heard of it? Their burgers are—"

Drake cleared his throat, interrupting Liam.

"Sorry, just wanted to see if you guys are ready? If you're still keen to do the major cavern, then we need to get going if we're gonna get you back before dinner time."

"We're keen," Liam said, standing up and brushing crumbs from his clothes. "Been looking forward to this for weeks."

"The major cavern?" Karen asked.

"Yeah, it's this giant pit off the main caves walk. You sail directly over it. Sounds cool, right?"

She began to nod as if she were a broken toy. "Cool. Cool. That sounds... cool. Right, no problem. Cool. Very cool."

I reached over, linking our fingers to give her a warm squeeze.

"Hey."

I waited until her gaze met mine.

"You got this. I'll be there the whole time."

For a moment, she seemed lost, unsure, then she nodded, sucking in a shaky breath. "Yeah. I got this. Thanks."

"Anytime."

And saying that made me realise that I wanted her to take me up on the offer.

5

Karen

"Oh, fuck no. Nooooo. Nope. No fucking way. Nope. Not happening. Fuck this. Seriously. No."

I stood with my back pressed against the cavern wall, the cool of the rock reassuring.

"Come on," Drake coaxed. "There's only one way out, and it's down. You did the rest of them. I promise this will be just as easy."

"I'm sorry, Drake. You're a really nice guy, but this is my home now. This is where I live." I lifted a hand to slap the rock behind me. "Just me, the cave and this very solid, very strong rock."

I heard sniggers from across the ledge and didn't have to turn to know it was Liam and Jay.

"Karrie—"

"Nope!" I shook my head fervently. "Will, you've sweet-talked me up to this point, but no more. I am a strong independent woman who is refusing to fall for your golden gaze. If this is the shelf I die on, then so be it. You're attractive, but unless you're prepared to get naked and rub oil all over yourself, then there is no fucking way I am moving from this spot."

Jay lost it, doubling over, his laughter echoing around the cavern.

"You know," Liam mused, tapping his cheek with one finger. "I reckon the old guy would do it if there was some baby oil around here."

Will flicked him the bird. "Shut the fuck up, Liam."

The kid grinned, his teeth flashing in the dim light. "Just saying."

"Shut it!" Will turned back to me, holding out a hand. "Come on, Karrie. You got this."

"I do not have this," I informed him primly. "I can assure you that if I get on this line, I will die. And if I die, that means I can't have dinner with you tomorrow night. So, your options are either allow me to die or allow me to live, and I might even let you visit."

Dane's shoulders began to shake, the strong, stoic man was actually laughing at me.

I don't care. Come hell or high water, I'm staying here.

"Look, I'm all for the low eco-living," Drake interjected, crouching before me. "But the thing is, you stay, we all stay. And the lights are on predetermined timers. They only stay on for a few hours a day. Now I'd be fine in the dark, but Dane here?" He pointed at his husband. "The man still needs a nightlight."

Dane snorted, rolling his eyes.

"So, your choice, Karen. We can all stay here and listen to Dane scream, or you can give it a go."

Will's fingers entwined with mine, his hand warm and solid. "No pressure."

I closed my eyes, sucking in deep, gulping breaths. "I hate this."

"I know. But you've done so well. One more obstacle, and that's it."

I tried to calm my racing heart. "Promise?"

"Swear it."

I nodded, keeping my eyes screwed shut. "Okay, I'm ready."

I heard Dane push off, heading down to the landing pad where he'd be waiting for us, trying desperately not to think about what was coming.

"What else is on this resolution list?" Will asked as Jay followed, hollering as he went.

"Skydiving."

Will snorted.

"Some kind of tantric yoga retreat."

"I thought that was a sex thing?"

I shrugged, my eyes still closed. "Maybe? Chrissy is desperate to get me laid."

Will muttered something under his breath. "And?"

"Meat load therapy. But Mistress H is doing that one."

"Is that a sex thing as well?" Will asked as Liam took off, letting out a 'yippee-ki-yay, motherfucker' shout.

"No, something to do with massages and rainforest noises. It's meant to be relaxing." I answered, still with my eyes closed.

The floor is solid. The floor is solid...

Will's hand settled between my shoulder blades, guiding me toward the zip line. "You want me to go first or after you?"

My hand shot out, finding his arm, fingernails digging in. "Don't you fucking leave me."

Will wrapped his arm around me, holding me close. "Don't worry, I got you."

As Drake quickly hitched me up, Will continued to soothe me, his voice warm and gentle.

"Ready, Karrie?"

I gulped, my eyes still squeezed shut.

"I don't know. Maybe?"

"Yes." Will squeezed my shoulders. "You are. And I'll be right behind you. Promise."

"Now?" Drake asked.

I nodded, gripping the handle on this one real tight. I sucked in a breath, leaned back, lifted my feet and—

"OH, MY FUCKING GAAAAAAWWWWWWWDDDDDDDD!" The shriek echoed through the cave, the giant gaping hole under my feet terrifying as I flew down the line.

"Yeah, Karen!"

"Go, Karrie!"

"You got it!"

The cheers rang in my ears as I forced my eyes open, staring at the walls as I raced down toward the small glow at the bottom.

I'm gonna die. I'm gonna die. I'm gonna—

A clip caught me, slowing my speed as Dane stepped up, catching me with a second loop and stopping me with a gentle jerk.

"You did it!" He held up a hand, and I automatically slapped it, looking back along the line for Will.

Jay and Liam crowded around, giving me high-fives and back slaps as we waited for Will to come down. The man did so quietly, grinning as he slid to a halt.

Will dropped to the ground, beaming at me. "Well done, Karen!"

I beamed, pumped up on endorphins. "Thank you! I couldn't have done it without you."

He wrapped me in a hug, giving me a tight squeeze. "Oh, you would have. It was all you."

Drake arrived, and, triumphant, we began the short trek back to the entry caves and out to the waiting minivan.

"You should join us for pizza," Jay said, dropping an arm around my shoulders. "The kids'll all be there, so it's a circus, but if you don't mind losing a finger or two, then we'd love to have you."

Will reached over, shoving Jay away. "He's joking. I try to break them of the biting habit the first week they arrive."

I grinned, dropping my voice so only Will could hear. "That's a shame. I don't mind a bit of rough."

As we stepped out into the afternoon light, I couldn't help but laugh at the red flush decorating his cheeks.

"So... pizza?"

"Love to."

6

Will

I've made a huge mistake.

Pizza and napkins flew about the table as my kids—young and old—devoured their meal. They were like ravenous animals, hissing and hollering over every bite.

"Dad, can I—"

"I've got time tomorrow to—"

"You're an idiot. I—"

The cacophony of sound blurred together to become a soundtrack to the moment I knew she'd leave. This woman who delighted and amused me and brought out every single protective instinct I possessed.

"I like your family," she said, leaning across

to snag a piece of pepperoni pizza. "They're a fun bunch."

Fun?

I looked around at the chaos, Jay flirting with the waitress, Liam tussling with Ryan, while Sam and Ash traded barbs.

"Fun?"

She laughed, throwing a hand out. "This is my definition of family."

"You're from a big one?"

She shook her head. "No. Just me. It was quiet but loving. My parents are retired now and live down south. I try to get down there every month or so to visit. They've taken up poker. I worry they're gonna fall in with a crime family."

I laughed, some of the tension leaving my shoulders. "You're game. The last woman I dated took one look at this lot and walked back out."

Karen lifted the pizza to her lips, her eyes sparkling. "I zip-line across cavernous black holes—your family doesn't frighten me."

I grinned, raising my cup and tipping it her way. "I'll cheers to that."

"Are you guys gonna kiss?"

Our heads twisted to see Sam watching us.

"Uh, no," I answered. "Don't worry, bud, we won't sully your young eyes at the dinner table."

He shrugged, fiddling with his straw. "It'd be okay, you know, if you wanted to. I wouldn't care."

Around us, the table quietened, all eyes falling on us.

"I don't know that this is the place for a kiss."

Jay leaned forward, his expression delighted. "Oh, come on, old man. You might not have many opportunities left. Time's a ticking—show your boys how it's done." He looked at Karen. "With the lady's permission first, of course."

"Of course," Karen laughed, rolling her eyes and turning to me. "Go on then."

Not how I expected tonight to go.

I leaned forward, cupping her cheek, searching her gaze for any sign she wasn't into this—instead, I found desire.

Fuck.

I leaned in, capturing her lips, expecting it to be a light kiss. I expected to keep it simple and chaste. After all, we were in a pizza parlour, and my kids were watching.

It was anything but.

She tasted like the finest scotch. Like base jumping and zip-lining. Like heaven and happiness and all the best fucking things. She tasted like home.

Fuck.

Her lips parted under mine, and I advanced, deepening our kiss, my tongue sliding against hers in a sensual move.

Her hands came up to fist my shirt, her head tilting back a fraction, inviting me to dig my fingers through her hair.

A cough sounded nearby.

We ignored it, lost in each other.

"Dad!"

I pulled back, breathing for a moment as I stared into Karen's eyes, our gaze locked.

I want you.

"And that, boys, is how it is *done,*" Jay said with a laugh. "Now I know where Hayden gets all his moves from. Kudos, Daddy-o! And to you, Ms. Karrie. You both are—" He made a sizzling sound. "—on fire!"

Karen blushed, ducking her head. "Maybe we could change the subject?"

I nodded, reluctantly letting her go. As she turned back to the table, allowing Jay to gently niggle her and giving back as good as she got, one thought played across my mind.

She's out of my league.

Karen

"And you kissed him?" Hannah asked, her eyes wide on the screen.

"Yep. And, spoiler, it was *good*." I grinned, completely unrepentant.

"Phew." Chrissy fanned a hand in front of her face, her expression dreamy. "Maybe I should take up zip-lining."

I cackled. "Yeah, sure. Maybe after the baby comes and you're not a billion months pregnant."

She waved a hand in my direction. "Details."

"Your turn Mistress H, how did the meat load therapy go?"

Hannah's rapt expression soured, her eyes

losing some of their spark. "Horrid. Christine, I blame you."

"For?"

Hannah dropped her head in her hands. "Everything."

A small message popped up on my screen.

CHRISSY

Uh-oh. This is serious, I've never seen Hannah like this before.

KAREN

Let me wield my magic.

"Mistress, do we need to make this a safe sharing corner?"

Hannah nodded, her head still in her hands.

"Alright, Wicked Women. Mistress H is asking for a safe space which means we're all here to support her. Shoot, Mistress."

Hannah sucked in a breath and then raised her head. "I might be attracted to someone. And he might not be attracted to me. In fact, I am certain he isn't."

"How are you certain?"

"He said so."

My eyebrows shot up. "I'm sorry?"

Hannah sighed, shaking her head. "It's a long story."

"And one I demand to know."

Hannah's lip trembled. "All I want is a family. Is that so much to ask?"

"Oh, H." I wrapped my arms around myself, nodding when she did the same. Hannah hated to be touched by anyone above the age of twelve. She struggled, finding the feeling overwhelming and threatening. It was why she'd trained as a BDSM mistress even if she wasn't into kink. She wanted the option to offer that to her future partner, to give to them a release without being forced to touch them.

I was still unpacking this one issue at a time.

She squeezed herself tight, closing her eyes. "There'd been a mix-up, he thought the therapy was a barbecue all-you-could-eat cookout. He was a good sport about it and stayed the entire time. But we saw each other naked. It was part of the therapy."

"Oh." Chrissy leaned forward. "Was he built?"

"No. He had a belly." Hannah's eyes blinked open, her expression stricken. "He said he's what they call strong-fat."

"And that distresses you?" I asked carefully.

"No. It's that I wanted to kiss his belly. I never want to kiss anything."

I swallowed a laugh. "I think you mean anyone. But let's return to the desire. You didn't like the feeling?"

"No, I did. I wanted to do it."

I cringed, suddenly connecting the dots. "Mistress... did you offer to kiss his belly?"

Hannah nodded glumly. "I said I was attracted to him. And that he was the first real man I'd ever been attracted to. I asked if I could kiss his belly and maybe other areas."

Chrissy and I both winced.

"And he said...?"

"That he was good. Then he turned and went into his meat hut, and that was the last I saw of him."

"Alright, we need to talk more about the meat huts but... Mistress, you get why he acted that way, right?"

Hannah nodded, her eyes sad. "I've analysed the situation and understand that I can't proposition people based on where I would like to kiss them."

I nodded. "Good. What will you do differently the next time this happens?"

She paused for a second, her eyes narrowing as she considered her options. "Perhaps offer to take him to dinner first?"

"Great! That's a great option."

Hannah nodded, then shook her head. "I should apologise. Do you think sending cookies would be well accepted?"

I looked at Chrissy on the chat, unsure what to say.

"Cookies are always a good option," Chrissy said in a tone that made it seem as if she were imparting some divine wisdom.

"Okay. Cookies it is."

A little bell rang in my ear.

"And on that note, that's it for our show today. If you'd like to know more about any of the adventures we did, check out our social media and website. In the meantime, have a nasty day."

I hit our theme song, bobbing my head in time to the music as the audio finished recording.

"Alright, we're clear."

"When do you see Will next?" Hannah asked me.

"Tonight." I felt my toes curl with anticipation. "We're going to dinner then checking out that dance class Chrissy signed us up for."

"Oh, you'll love it. Mae is wonderful. She also teaches kids." Chrissy patted her belly. "I expect this little one to be tapping in her class shortly."

I rolled my eyes. "So much expectation on such a little person. You better be careful with that one, Chris."

She laughed. "Never! Only the best for my one and only."

"Never say never." Even as the words rolled off my tongue, I realised they also applied to me.

Well. Who would have thought I could find love in a cave? It would make for a hell of an anniversary story.

I grinned.

8

Will

I hovered in front of Karen's door, nervousness making me anxious.

Wallet. Car keys. Cell. Kids are at friends for the night. I brushed my teeth and put on deodorant. Dinner reservations are confirmed. Fuck. What am I missing?

My phone buzzed and I pulled it out, swiping to read the message posted in the group chat from Hayden.

DOGG PACK CHAT
DR.DOGG

Dad, I love you, but for the love of all that is holy, make sure you use a condom. No one wants a repeat of your misspent youth.

JAYWOOD

Especially us. I mean, we
definitely don't want a Hayden2.0

DR.DOGG

You wish you could be this cool,
Woody.

ASH

Can you guys cool it with the
condom talk? I don't want to
have to explain the birds and
bees to an 8yr old.

SAMTHEPUP

What's a condom?

ASH

Oh, great. Thanks a lot, you guys.

RYAN

Dad, what I think we're all trying
to say is we love you and
have fun.

JAMES

Speak for yourself. I just hope he
gets laid. Don't worry, Dad. We
won't wait up!

I sighed, running a hand over my face, exasperated and amused in equal measure.

DADDYDOGG

Sam, I'll tell you when you get home tomorrow. Now go play with your friends. Ash, don't explain anything. Ryan, thank you for the vote of confidence. James, Jay, and Hayden... *facepalm emoji*

JAYWOOD

Kissy face emoji

DR.DOGG

Love heart emoji

JAMES

Eggplant emoji

DADDYDOGG

Just wait till you all have kids of your own.... Good night boys. Love you.

I slid the phone back into my pocket and rapped a knuckle against Karen's door.

I'd half expected her to ghost me. I wouldn't have even blamed her. Taking on a divorcee with six kids would be a lot for anyone.

The door opened, revealing a woman I could only describe as perfect.

She wore an eggplant purple wrap sweater dress that hugged her just right. Her tiny stature had been elevated thanks to spiked heels on her feet. Her hair had been pulled back into some kind of soft top-knot, while her eyes were somehow bigger and darker, her lips fuller and painted a deep crimson.

"Hey, Will! You look great. Let me just grab my coat, and we can go." Karen left the door open, turning to pull a black coat off a rack by the door, giving me a side profile.

Dinner. Must get to dinner. Must get to—

My control snapped when she bent over, picking something up from the floor, the curve of her ass pressing against her dress.

Fuck dinner. We can eat later.

She stood, and I approached, wrapping her in my arms and claiming her mouth.

"Gotta taste you," I grunted, desperate for another chance to memorise her flavour. Karen melted against me, her mouth opening, her body glorious against mine.

We kissed for a moment, feasting on each other's mouth, desperate and needy, her little whimpers feeding my grunts.

"Dinner," I said, attempting to step back, to be a gentleman.

"Fuck dinner." Karen reached up, fisting my hair, dragging my mouth back down to meet hers. "Dinner is for the weak."

I chuckled, then groaned as her hand

snaked between us, cupping my erection through the material of my slacks.

Fuck. Fuck. Fuck! Keep it together, Will.

"Bedroom. Hurry."

I gave in, surrendering to her desperate plea. I bent and lifted her up, carrying her down the hall.

"Where?" I asked, barely able to grunt the word as my body ached to be in her. Now.

"Third on the left."

I staggered down, pausing to press her against the wall and fuck her mouth with my tongue. A poor imitation of what I wanted to do, but the best I could do at that moment.

In the bedroom, I laid her on the bed, stepping back to push the skirt of her dress up, a sound ripping from my throat.

"Oh, fuck, Karrie." I dropped to my knees, my hands parting her thighs. "You're fucking gorgeous."

With deliberate intent, my head dipped, my tongue finding her damp panties, seeking her clit through the wet fabric.

"Oh, my Gods!" Karen grasped my hair, pressing me closer, wiggling as my mouth teased her through the material. "More!"

As my lady wishes.

I hooked a finger pulling aside her panties,

too impatient and desperate to pull away. Under me, she arched, pressing her core closer to my mouth, an offering.

I'm going to destroy all your fantasies.

With lips, tongue, and fingers I purposefully drove her wild, dancing them across her sensitive flesh, pushing her higher and higher but never allowing her to break.

Your pleasure is mine.

"Please!" she begged when I withdrew, pulling back, denying her another orgasm. "Will!"

I stood, hands dropping as I slowly began to unbuckle my pants. "You want me, baby?"

Her eyes fluttered open, her gaze dropping to my crotch as I began to unzip my fly. Her tongue darted out, licking her lips, and I teased us both, slowly gliding the zip down.

"Holy mother of...." Her voice trailed off as I shoved my pants and briefs down, revealing my cock.

I couldn't deny her reaction certainly felt good.

"You want this?" I asked, fisting my dick.

"Yes," she admitted, watching me with hungry eyes as I teased my cock, giving a long, slow tug.

"Good."

Pre-cum glistening in the dim light, my thumb catching the drop and using it to help ease my glide. Her lips parted, and suddenly I wanted her mouth around my dick.

"You gonna kiss this cock, baby?"

"Yes." Her answer sounded breathy, eager. And it did strange things to me.

I surged up on the bed, hovering over her, my cock positioned at her mouth. With a happy sigh, Karen reached out, her small hand wrapping around my member, her generous curves still hidden from my view.

Fucking shame. Next time take off her dress first.

My brain short-circuited after that thought as her lips wrapped around my dick.

"Fuck, fuck, fuck," I chanted, fighting the urge to pump into her mouth. "Your mouth is phenomenal. You're phenomenal. Fuck. Fuck. Fuck. Fuuuuck."

I had to stop, had to escape her hot mouth if I stood any chance of getting the opportunity to make love to her.

I pulled back, my control nearly snapping at her whimpered protest.

"Shh." I pressed kisses to her mouth. "You keep that up, and this will be over far too soon."

Karen wiggled under me, removing her panties. "Well, guess we better get comfortable then."

With fumbling fingers and a few giggles, we stripped each other, our lips and hands worshipping every newly revealed inch of skin.

"Oh," she whispered as her hands glided over the bulk of my chest. "You're perfect."

I cupped her breasts, lowering my head to press hot, sucking kisses to their tips. "I could say the same for you."

I trailed up and down her body, my mouth and hands alternating as I mapped her pleasure. Perhaps it would take me three years. Perhaps it would take me thirty, but I had never in my life wanted anything more than I wanted this moment. The moment when she would shake and scream under me as I drew from her a powerful orgasm.

"Can't wait," she panted, her body beginning to undulate under mine. "Please, Will."

Condom. Fuck. Where's a condom?

"Condom?" I asked, panting heavily.

"Second drawer."

I reached over, finding a dusty packet, no doubt expired judging by the picture on the box.

Do condoms expire? Fuck it. This'll have to do.

I rolled one on, gaze locked on Karen as she watched me through half-lidded eyes.

"Let me please you."

I found her core, sliding fingers through her slick heat, finding her wet and ready.

"Karrie," I groaned. "So. Fucking. Wet."

"I've been horny all day," she admitted, red flushing her cheeks. "I kept thinking of that kiss."

"Same."

Our eyes met, and I leaned in, my cock pressing against her.

"Ready?"

She nodded. "Yes."

We both groaned as I filled her, her tight pussy gripping me.

Tight, hot, wet—fucking perfect.

"Been a while," she muttered, her little pants driving me wild. "Gods, this feels so good."

"Fucking brilliant," I agreed, beginning to move.

We fucked. Dirty, hard, and punishingly good. Our bodies two halves of the same deeply erotic whole. For a moment, I couldn't figure out where I ended, and she began. Then she came, her body milking my cock, locked together as we made filthy love.

"Fuck! Karrie!" I emptied myself in her. Desire and despair warring as I collapsed on top of her.

Fuck. That was too quick. Shit.

We lay like that, our bodies still joined, our hearts thumping wildly. Then I rolled us, settling us on our sides.

"Sorry." I reached out, brushing a stray hair from her cheek. "I wasn't planning on doing that."

She grinned, her cheeks still flushed. "You weren't? That's a shame."

I felt myself relax, finding an answering grin. "It's just that you're fucking perfect, Karen. I wanted to make tonight perfect for you."

She leaned forward, pressing a kiss to my shoulder. "I got laid by a man I deeply respect and am overwhelmingly attracted to. I'm pretty sure this *is* perfect."

Any residual tension left my body.

"I mean.... Unless he wants to make it extra perfect by going another round?"

I grinned at her hopeful expression. "You don't need dinner?"

"Maybe later. This—" She reached down, giving my cock a loving stroke. "—seems to be the more pressing need."

I found myself rallying, my cock becoming hard once more.

"Mm, I think I might have another round or two in me."

I rolled onto her, covering her glorious fullness with my body, revelling in the soft peaks and dips of her as we made love—three additional times.

When I woke the next morning, I was pretty sure my cock was broken. But as my sons would say—totally worth it.

9

Karen

I spread my arms out, pointing at the school of fish.

Beside me, Will shot me a thumbs up, his body stilling as we watched the beautiful sea life swim past us.

Above us, his youngest son, Sam, swam around with his brothers, their legs just visible in the sun-dappled water.

A turtle appeared from the seafloor, lazily gliding past us on her way to some important date. She glanced my way as she passed by, giving me one long, slow blink.

A perfect day.

Apart from the difficulties of finding a wet suit in my size and throwing myself backward over the side of a boat, scuba diving was quickly becoming a pastime I wouldn't mind taking up. Between the amazing sea life, the cool dive wrecks, and Will—it felt almost like a celebration.

The dive instructor swam my way, signalling it was time to begin our ascent. Over the next forty minutes, we swam slowly higher, circling, acclimatising ourselves to the changing pressure and oxygenation, and then continuing upward.

As we burst through the surface, the instructor gestured that we could take our breathing masks off.

"That was incredible! Can I come back next weekend?" I enthused, dipping the mask in the water to clean off my spit.

"I'm a fan," Will agreed. "Did you see that turtle? She was massive."

"He," the instructor, a woman named Ruth, corrected. "That was old Fred. He's a regular around here. Grandfathered most of the turtles along this side of the cove."

"You know, I'm not sure why I never tried this before today." I tread water, shaking my head. "I live by the ocean, and the most I normally do is go for a walk along the rock pools."

Ruth grinned. "Most people do that. It's why Drake and Dane started this. When the marina was finally complete, they saw it as a chance for people to experience marine life as it should be experienced."

"Wild, oxygenated, and stuffed into a wet suit?" I asked with a grin.

"Exactly!" Ruth laughed. "Come on, your boys are waiting. Let's get you home."

I scrambled onto the back of the yacht, grunting and groaning as I slipped and slid, heaving my body up and over.

"So graceful," I muttered, flopping onto my back. "Such poise."

"Karrie?"

I tilted my head back, grinning up at Sam.

Over the last few weeks, Will and I had become fixtures in each other's life. It was as if we were magnets—polar opposites yet when we were put together, nothing could separate us.

And, lucky for me, his family had embraced me with their whole hearts. Will had met my parents, and we'd had lunch with Hayden when he'd come into town to visit. I'd never felt more accepted.

"Yeah, kid?"

"Can I come next time?"

"When you're ten," I reminded him gently, gratefully accepting his offered hand. "But I promise, the moment you're ten, you and me, we're gonna go down and see the pirate ship."

"Swear?"

I nodded solemnly, crossing my heart and holding out my hand, my pinky cocked. "Pinky swear."

He linked his pinky with mine, giving it a shake. "Cool."

I hip-checked him. "Come on, let's eat."

Over lunch, Will and I regaled the boys with stories of what we'd seen while Ruth drove the boat, taking us back to the Capricorn Cove marina.

"You want the rest of my sandwich?" I asked Ryan, offering him the chicken club.

"You sure?" he asked, eyeing the delicious morsel.

"Yeah." I patted my stomach as we hit another small wave. "This rocking isn't sitting well with me."

"Thanks!" The teenager stuffed half of it in his mouth, chewing enthusiastically as we listened to Will describe the wreck for Sam.

Will's eyes met mine across the boat, his gaze warm and concerned. I waved him off, communicating without words that I was fine.

I twisted, tilting my head back, allowing the sea breeze to blow through my hair.

I'd never been in a relationship where I felt so at ease. There wasn't anything hard about this. We just clicked. Ever since the caves, Will had become my cheerleader and supporter. We finished each other's sentences, we laughed without saying a word, I sometimes found myself handing him something before he'd even asked for it.

This kind of instant connection was the type of thing I read about in books, not something that I'd ever expected to experience.

And yet, here I was. Living it. Living an actual love story.

My stomach jumped, my mouth filling with saliva as I twisted, bending over to puke over the side of the boat.

Well damn.

Will was immediately there, brushing back my hair, holding me as I retched.

"I got you," he soothed. "Sam, can you get Karrie a bottle of water?"

"On it, Dad."

I closed my eyes, my cheeks flushing with embarrassment. "I have no idea what's gotten into me. I was fine on the way out, and it's way less choppy now."

Will shrugged, hands still soothing over my hair. "You're fine. Don't worry about it."

But back on land, the nausea didn't abate. A day passed, then two, with the nausea continuing.

"That's it, I'm taking you to the hospital,"

Will declared on Tuesday morning. He stood in my doorway, hands-on-hips as he stared down at me curled around the toilet bowl.

"It's just a gastro bug," I protested weakly. "I'll be fine."

"Hush. We'll let the doctors work it out."

With a resigned sigh, I allowed him to help me change, piling me into the car and driving me down to the local clinic for testing.

"Could be the bends," the doctor remarked when we finally got in to see him. "Not common, but if you've been scuba diving, then we need to rule it out. No chance of pregnancy?"

"No, I'm over forty."

The doctor grinned. "And sexually active, I assume?"

"I mean, sure." I shrugged. "But we use protection."

"Mm, what type?"

I froze, my eyes widening as I rapidly began to count back.

"Oh. My. God. Will... the condoms."

Will's head twisted, his hands coming up to frame my face. "No, it can't be. We've been using them religiously."

I gulped then gulped again. "They were old. I didn't think they expired. But... my period... it's been over a month. I'm late. I'm *never* late. And I'm not on anything."

The doctor reached into a drawer, pulling out a test kit. "Here. Let's at least rule it out."

Fifteen minutes later, we stood over the pee stick, staring at the results window.

+ POSITIVE

"But... how?" I whispered, shocked to my core.

The doctor chuckled.

"Sorry, I mean, I get *how* but not... how? I'm forty-two. I didn't think...." I placed a hand on my belly. "I never thought I'd have a chance. I'm old."

"It will be a geriatric pregnancy," the doctor agreed. "As you get older, there are more risks. But I'll write a referral for a wonderful obstetrician, and we'll make sure you're all set." He made a note on the chart. "We'll still do some tests to rule out anything else, but I'm gonna guess your nausea is morning sickness. I'll prescribe some anti-nausea medication, but the best option is to rest, drink some ginger tea, and try to keep your fluids up."

He left the room, leaving Will and me alone.

"Wow," I stared at him. "A baby. Our baby. I can't.... Thoughts? Facts? Opinions?"

He looked shell-shocked, his mouth opening and closing a few times before he cleared his throat. "I...."

I waited, expecting him to continue.

"It's just...."

I smiled encouragingly.

"I thought Sam would be my last."

I froze, feeling as if a bucket of cold water had been tipped over me.

"What does that mean, Will?"

"It's...nothing, it's just a shock. That's all."

I swallowed, nausea once again rising. "Are you saying you don't want this?"

"No, it's just—"

"Hello, mommy and daddy-to-be!" The nurse bustled in, interrupting our conversation. "I'm just here to take some blood. I won't be a moment."

Will stepped back. "I need to make a call. Are you cool by yourself for a minute?"

I nodded, feeling something within me break. "Sure."

He left, not offering even a backward glance.

I looked down at my stomach, tears stinging the backs of my eyes.

Don't worry, baby. I want you.

10

Will

"Can I help you?" the ancient woman in the hospital gift store asked.

"Um, maybe?"

She grinned, tucking a chunk of electric blue hair behind her ear. "What's the occasion? Birth, cancer-free diagnosis?"

"How did you know it's a celebration?"

She laughed. "I've worked here fifty years. You learn to pick the body language."

"Birth. Or, more precisely, impending birth."

"And you want to get her something special?"

I nodded. "I... she's the love of my life. I've never felt this way about anyone before." I held up the congratulations teddy bear. "This doesn't seem special enough."

"Come this way."

She stepped behind the counter, bending to unlock a drawer and pull out a small tray from the secure case. She placed it on the counter, sliding the lid off.

"Rings and necklaces. We only carry a small number because not many people buy them, but I figure we carry some for moments such as this one."

She tapped the drawer. "I work with a local jeweller. They're all certified and—"

"That one." I reached over, running my thumb over the engagement ring.

"Good choice," she said with approval. "Rose gold, with sapphire and diamonds. The geometric cut is unusual but I can give you the name of the jeweller, she's local and can help with designing a matching wedding band."

"That'd be perfect, thanks."

Heart hammering in my chest, I pulled out my phone, snapped a picture of the ring and popped it into family chat.

DADDYDOGG

Boys, speak now or forever hold your peace. I'm marrying Karen.

SAMTHEPUP

Yay!

ASH

About time.

JAYWOOD

I called it. Pretty sure Liam owes me ten bucks.

RYAN

Congratulations, Dad. You and Karrie deserve all the happiness!

JAMES

Does that mean we get to call her mum? Tell her I'm down for that if she doesn't mind.

DR.DOGG

You sly dog. Well done old man! Has she said yes yet?

I gulped back tears as the woman packaged the ring, overwhelmed with love for my boys.

DADDYDOGG

Not yet. Haven't asked. Will let you know.

SAMTHEPUP

If she says no tell her I'll help her do the dishes every night for a month.

ASH

Holy shit! That's a proposal she can't refuse. Sam doesn't do ANYTHING.

SAMTHEPUP

Hey!

I slid the phone back into my pocket, paid for the ring then strode back to Karen's room.
This is happening. I found my person.
Taking a deep breath, I stepped inside.

11

Karen

I couldn't stop crying.

Can I blame it on the baby yet? Or is that too much of a cop-out too soon?

The tears had started after the nurse had left with my blood vials and Will hadn't returned. Big, gut-wrenching sobs shook my whole body.

I can't believe he left.

My heart felt as if it were breaking. If I hadn't known I was in love with Will before, I definitely knew now.

You love him.

And he doesn't want you. Or the baby. He's got six kids, Karrie.

Wait, no. You can't refer to yourself as Karrie

anymore. That's too much of a reminder of all you've lost.

I hunched over, pressing a tissue to my eyes, my sobs coming harder.

"What the fuck?" Will's hands settled on my shoulders, sliding across to pull me close. "Karen! What's happened? Jesus."

I pulled back, unsure if this was a figment of my imagination or if I was having a mental breakdown.

"W-W-W- Will?"

"I'm here, baby. Jesus, what the fuck? Talk to me."

The sobs continued; my body confused by his presence.

Why is he here?

"W-w-why are you h-h-here?" I hiccupped, scrubbing at my tears.

"What? Of course, I'm here. Where the fuck else would I be?"

I drew in a shuddering breath. "You're n-n-not leaving m-m-me?"

His eyebrows shot up; his expression startled. "What the ever-loving fuck? No!"

Happiness the likes of which I'd never known burst over me. All tension released from my body, the sobs of heartbreak immediately turning into tears of joy.

"Oh, baby." He wrapped me tight, crushing me to his chest as I cried.

"Ms. Quim—oh! I'm so sorry. Is there anything I can—?"

"Just give us a minute," Will said softly, over my head.

"Of course." The nurse stepped out, shutting the door to the examination room.

He murmured soothingly as I cried it all out. The fear, the joy, the love, the bittersweet heartache of loving someone and fearing they were lost to you. All of it came streaming out leaving me a snotty, damp, wrung-out mess.

"Better?" he asked when the hiccups subsided.

I nodded, sniffing a little.

"I know this isn't romantic. I expect you had visions in your head of roses and candle-lit dinners, or maybe something involving sky jumping at the rate you're going." His smile reached his eyes, crinkling the wrinkles that lived there.

God, he really is the most handsome of men.

"But I find I can't live another moment without you, Karrie." Will dropped to one knee, digging in his pocket to pull out a small square box. "Marry me. Marry me and let me love you. Let me love you and our baby, and have a life with you both. Please."

I gasped, my heart thundering as I stared at him. "But... is this... you don't have to. We can co-parent without—"

He shook his head fervently. "No. It's not because of the baby. It's because of you. You're everything I've ever wanted. From the first moment I saw your butt in those Yoda pants—"

"Hey! You said you didn't look!"

"—to this moment right here. Every single second with you is perfection. It's always going to be perfection. Even if we're fighting or crying or kissing. Every second with you is my heart's wish. I love you, Karen. I want to marry you, not for the baby, but for me. The baby is icing on an already decadent cake."

I sniffed, tears threatening to spill again. "Are you sure?"

He grinned. "I've never been more sure of anything in my life."

"Then yes. Hell, yes!"

He surged to his feet, his hands coming to cup my face as he pressed joyous, hungry kisses across my cheeks, my lips, and my forehead. "I love you. I fucking love you."

"I love you too." I wept, overwhelmed by all the feelings inside me. "But we're not getting married until after the baby."

"Whatever you want," he agreed.

Our lips met, our tongues tangling as we

pressed into each other, breathing in the same air, a meeting of two souls.

"Well, I can see I don't need to explain how this happened." The doctor's amused comment interrupted our make-out session.

He tapped his clipboard. "You're cleared to head home. Bloods look great. I've written a referral for the obstetrician and managed to get you an appointment for Friday but all looks great. They'll schedule a scan to be sure. In the meantime, fluids and bed rest. Hopefully, the nausea improves."

"Thanks, doc." Will held out a hand, shaking the doctor's enthusiastically. "Thanks for everything."

The doctor grinned. "It's news like this that brightens my day. Now get outta here you love birds."

And with a laugh, we did just that.

EPILOGUE 1

Karen

Nine months later

"Push!"

I screwed my eyes closed, sucking in a breath as I fought the pain.

"Again! One, two, three, push!"

With a last shove, Chrissy and I wrestled the new bed into place.

"Jesus," I muttered, wiping at the sweat on my brow. "We really should have waited for the guys to get home."

Chrissy waved a hand. "Why wait when we can get the job done?"

"'Cause I'm a month postpartum and

shouldn't be doing this kind of strenuous work?" I said with an eyebrow raise.

"If our peasant foremothers could return to sowing potatoes in fields and running from marauding English after having babies, surely we can handle one little bed."

"I don't know how to answer that."

She grinned. "Anyway, Amy is gonna love it."

I looked around the little girl's room, grinning at the ballerina mice on the wall. "She really is."

Amy happened to be barely a year old but already acted like she was going on twenty-six. Chrissy had her hands full with her daughter.

My phone buzzed, interrupting my thoughts.

DADDYDOGG

How's my baby?

MOMMYDOGG

Me or your offspring?

DADDYDOGG

You, of course. I already know my little girl is perfect.

I chuckled, loving Will's utter devotion to our children.

MOMMYDOGG

We're both good. Probably another fifteen minutes, if you want to come pick us up?

DADDYDOGG

I'm on my way. Love you.

MOMMYDOGG

Love you too.

I made chit-chat with Chrissy, tossing around some ideas for the podcast as we watched our babies nap.

"Aren't they precious?" Chrissy whispered in a lull. "I never thought I'd love someone so fiercely. It's like I'm actually afraid I'll lock her up and never let her out of my sight."

I chuckled. "I get it."

Chrissy eyed me. "Are you happy, Karrie?"

I looked down at my precious daughter, thinking about the sleepless nights since Janeane's birth, the discomfort of pregnancy, the constant worry. I thought about the boys and the adjustment it'd taken for them, having a pregnant woman in their space.

Then I thought about my fiancé. I thought about Will's wrinkles and salt-and-pepper hair. I thought about his laugh and the way he held me close. I thought about his fingers as they rubbed my feet. And his cock as he fucked me until we both came.

And I thought about how full and wonderful my life had become. How I no longer lived in front of a computer screen or behind a microphone.

"Oh yes." I reached out, tracing a hand over my daughter's tiny cheek. "In my wildest dreams, I couldn't imagine this level of happy."

Chrissy sighed dreamily. "And to think, I started it all."

I stared at her for a beat then burst out laughing.

EPILOGUE 2

Karen

Ten years later

"Whose idea was this!?" I yelled over the sound of the screaming wind. "Yours! Remember?"

I gulped, closing my eyes. "If I ever do have an idea like this again—stop me!"

Will laughed, reaching out a hand to capture mine, giving me a reassuring squeeze. "We can do this!"

"Ready?" The skydiving instructor called. "On my mark, three, two, one."

The first of our party leapt from the perfectly safe plane, free-falling toward the ground. *OH MY FUCKING GOD!*

I gulped, gasping for air, panic swamping me as the next student jumped from the plane.

"Ready?" The instructor I was strapped to asked.

"No!" I yelped, shaking my head. "No way, no how."

Will shot me a grin from his place beside me. "You got this, Karrie. I'll see you on the ground."

With that, he and the instructor he'd been strapped to leap from the plane, leaving me and my guy as the last to leave.

"Come on." He shuffled us to the door, pausing for a moment as my feet dangled into the sky.

"OH GOD!" I screeched, my words snatched by the air. "OH JESUS!"

With a shove, we were falling, flying through the air, dropping at such speed I got a free facelift.

Words were coming from my mouth, no doubt expressions of utter horror as we fell but any sound had been ripped away, replaced by the roar of air as it rushed past.

We joined the others in the group, forming a rough circle as we fell.

My eyes met Will's across the group, his grin wide and joyous.

Skydiving had to be of the devil, and I hated

every single thing about this moment... except him. His joy was infectious, and I ignored the pit in my belly and the whispering words which said I was about to die, instead concentrating on my husband.

Each year on the anniversary of our meeting, he packed me up, and we did something crazy in celebration. It'd taken him ten years, but finally, he'd convinced me to do this.

He shot me thumbs up, and I flicked him the bird, laughter bubbling up.

I loved him. More than loved him. I was in active love with him. Every day falling deeper, learning something new about him, something that shifted our relationship, burying more roots, entwining us more closely.

He had more salt than pepper these days. More wrinkles and laugh lines. But ten years and he was still the most attractive, sexy, loving man I'd ever known.

The instructor pulled the strap, our parachute opening to jerk us up, slowing our descent.

"What did you think?" he asked as the air calmed, and I could finally begin to hear again.

"I think I'm going to kill my husband, and no court in the land would convict me."

He cackled, pointing to the blue parachute

in the distance. "That's him. Shall we race him to the ground?"

"Let's."

The view may have been spectacular, and I may enjoy the endorphins racing through my body, but there was nothing in the world quite like standing on solid ground.

I dropped to my knees, pressing my hands against the grass as Will walked up.

"Never again," I declared, running my palm over the grass. "Honestly, Will. Never, ever again."

"Do you remember that first anniversary? You made me go to a tantric massage retreat."

I rolled my eyes. "Yes, 'cause tantric massage is comparable to jumping out of a perfectly safe plane."

"Karrie, we weren't allowed to have sex for a week. Don't you remember that? It was meant to be our anniversary!"

I laughed, allowing him to help me up. "Pretty sure we broke that rule on day one."

"And day two," he said with a grin, wrapping an arm around me.

"And maybe day three through seven."

We grinned

"I wouldn't have done this if not for you." I leaned into him. "You push me to do wild stuff, Mr. Dogg."

"And you push me to be a better man."

I tilted my head back, grinning up at him. "Not sure that's true."

"Oh, it is." He leaned down, capturing my lips, the kiss turning filthy very quickly.

With a sigh, I pulled back, resting my head on his chest. "Speaking of adventure...."

"Mm?"

"Let's go make love in the parking lot."

Will burst out laughing, burying his head in my hair. "Fuck, I love you."

"I fucking love you too. Now ravish me, Will. Your wife requests it."

And later, after we finally recovered my bra from between the backseats, we drove home to our little family and lived happily ever after.

~

My dearest greedy readers, thank you so much for reading Will and Karen's story. You can grab the bonus slice of life on my website.

You can continue the entire series, or start the Dogg Pack series featuring Will's adopted sons at www.EvieMitchell.com

If you enter the code EBOOK10 you can get 10% off your purchase from my website.

Be sure to also sign up for my newsletter or check out my website for more book news.

ABOUT THE AUTHOR

Evie Mitchell is a thirty-something romance author (she/her/hers) living with disability. She believes in inclusion, accessibility, and fierce romance. Her loves include steamy romance novels, her husband, their THREE sausage dogs (heaven help her), and her ever-growing collection of book-related mugs.

As a woman with a diverse work history including in areas such as emergency response, event management, human rights, disability access, and security - her books are filled with true stories (bridezillas), worst-case scenarios (malfunctioning dresses), and her favorite tropes (one-bed).

Evie specialises in fiercely inclusive happily ever afters.

ALSO BY EVIE MITCHELL

Capricorn Cove Series

The Shake-Up

Double the D

Muffin Top

The Mrs. Clause

New Year Knew You

Double Breasted

As You Wish

You Sleigh Me

Resolution Revolution

Meat Load

Larsson Siblings Series

Thunder Thighs

Clean Sweep

The X-list

Reality Check

The Christmas Contract

Dogg Pack Books

Puppy Love

Bad English

The Frock Up

Pier Pressure

All Access Series

Knot My Type

Love Flushed

Nameless Souls MC Series

Runner

Wrath

Ghost

Shield

Elliot Security Series

Rough Edge

Bleeding Edge